CW00382333

These Two Roses

Sana Nassari

Translated by Alireza Abiz

To Ali, for his love and patience

CONTENTS

These Two Roses

The Jeep was on a bumpy road. The middle-aged man sitting in the back turned around and pushed aside the corner of the canvas cover. Beyond the filthy plastic behind the cover, the remnants of the day seemed more depressing to him. The entire windshield was rubbed with mud, except for a small circle for the driver's vision, through which the dull light of dusk lit his face giving it a peculiar innocence. He was determined to take his friend to a safe place. He had put his friend's head on his lap. Blood had dried on the temple hair. The man dropped the canvas, it got dark. He turned around and sat up straight. The corpse's hand was drooping. The man closed his eyes. The corpse was coiled up in the seat. The man leaned his head against the back of the seat. The tremors gradually subsided. There was no sound from outside, except for the sound of the Jeep's engine. Passengers were sitting compactly, and the rest of the space was filled with boxes, empty and full.

The boy asked the man, "don't you see them in your dreams?"

The man was shocked. He turned to the boy sitting next to him and said, "Don't I see who?"

"Your kids!"

The man closed his eyes to visualize his daughter's smiling face, but he saw his wife gently tucking a strand of hair behind her ear. The children slept early, and the woman read books until late. The man would approach her. His wife would notice him. She would put a sign next to the pages and close the book. Her black hair sparkled. The man would whisper something under her ear and sniff her neck. The perfume wrapped around his nose. He pressed his eyelids together, squeezed, and suddenly opened his eyes to clear his mind. A faint light illuminated the air and made the young figure visible, then again, the grey mist covered everyone. The man regained his stony composure and said, "No."

"But I dream about all my clan," said the boy. "My mother, my father, my brothers, my sisters' children, my sisters' husbands, everyone, everyone... It's as if I spend my days here and my nights at home."

The man said, "Hmm."

The boy laughed for no reason and tapped his leg. The bulky man who was sleeping on the other side of the boy moved but did not wake up. The boy was still laughing, shaking his head left and right.

"Ask me what I dreamed of last night", he said.

But he didn't wait for an answer.

"I dreamed that my mother had made a tandoori hilsa fish and we are sitting at a big table. Then someone came and said that the toilet well is full, and we need to empty it. They say if you need to go to the toilet while asleep, you always dream of a toilet, for sure."

The man thought of his wife's last letter.

The doctor had said, "Madam! People are being killed on the front lines in hundreds every day, urinary incontinence..." The woman had said, "Shush!" but it was too late. Her son, embarrassed, had got up from the hospital bench and quietly gone to the yard. That evening, the woman was taking the children to the park to play when an airplane flew overhead. His son said he wanted to be a pilot. When they arrived at the park, a war song could be heard from the loudspeakers. A large crowd had gathered there around a tank. A group of children were on top of the tank and looked very happy. A stranger helped their son mount the tank. That night he did not sleep until late in the excitement of seeing a real tank.

Their son got out of the tank and disappeared amidst the black chadors of women. The woman pulled the girl's hand and sped up. For a moment, she saw the chequered shirt of her son and lost it again. The surrounding gazebos were constantly filled and emptied of visitors. Tents with field hospital decor. Beds and stretchers and anti-chemical masks and replicas of wounded fighters in real body dimensions. The woman peeped in. Her son was standing by an oxygen cylinder, opening and closing its valve. Children of the same age had lined up for a young man wearing a white uniform to listen to their heartbeats with a stethoscope. The boy saw one of his classmates and joined the queue. The woman took a deep breath and her lungs filled with the stuffy air. Her body under the clothes was soaked with sweat. The girl pulled her hand out of her mother's and stood a few steps away, next to the bed. The woman tightened the scarf clip under her chin. Her heart sank as she heard the mourning songs from the loudspeakers. The boy came out of the line and said, "Let's go." The woman took both children by the hand to leave, but the girl didn't move. She raised her head. Large drops of tears flowed down her cheeks, which were red from the heat. "Dad," she said, pointing to the dummy on the bed. The woman turned back astonished. The dummy bore no resemblance to her husband.

"It's not Daddy, my dear..."

A sharp pain stabbed at her chest. She crouched next to the girl.

"Yes, it's Dad"

She hugged the girl and stood up. She took her small hand to touch the hard body of the dummy.

"It's a sculpture, dear. See!"

The young man shouted, "Don't touch, ma'am. Children don't understand but it's like the adults are even worse".

The woman felt like crying. The boy pulled her chador.

"Let's go. Mom let's goooo".

And he twisted his body.

"I need to pee, please let's go".

Betadine had been poured on the left pocket of the dummy's green uniform. It looked like he had been shot in his heart.

"It's Daddy. He is asleep", her daughter said.

The woman could not hold back her tears. Her chin must have trembled first, and then a muffled sound in her throat followed by a relentless flood of tears. She has written that she couldn't sleep till morning.

The boy said to the middle-aged man, "Alright! Alright, don't be so pensive. How old are they?"

The man missed home and felt a strong urge to see his wife, to see his children. His heart pounded.

"You talk so much nonsense," said the bulky man while stretching his body.

"What?!" Said the boy: "You've been sleeping like a corpse."

"One is seven and the other one is three years old," the man said.

The bulky man said, "You didn't let me sleep a minute, dammit".

The boy said, "Okay, it's my fault. You're right, you're right!"

"Fuck off," said the bulky man.

And scratched his beard. He kept poking the boy in the arm with his elbow.

The boy turned to the man and said, "See?"

The man thought he shouldn't have left without his backpack. At least he could have brought along the letter. The Jeep sputtered and stalled. They got out. The sun was setting behind intertwined purple clouds. Somewhere far away, something was burning, and a column of smoke was rolling upwards. The man took a few steps forward. There was no moving object in sight throughout the desert. He felt lightheaded. The driver got out and opened the bonnet. The boy arrived at the first Iraqi corpse which was lying on its stomach. He reached out and unclasped its wristwatch. The bulky man got out of the Jeep. He had his uniform unbuttoned till his chest. He approached the driver and asked reproachfully, "We are stuck in the desert, aren't we?"

The man walked away. Only an orange line was left from the sun behind the darkening horizon, which was fading bit by bit. His wife didn't want their son to become a pilot. He tried to remember every word exactly as his wife had written in the letter. He wanted to remember every single word. The boy reached the man who hadn't noticed he was standing over a corpse. The boy slightly pulled back one sleeve. There was no watch. He pulled back the other sleeve. The corpse did not have a hand. Instead of the wrist, there was a small mass of scar tissue healed years ago. The man hit the ground with the tip of his boot. Dust rose a little and dispersed in the air. The boy sat down. Blood had dried on the left pocket of the corpse's uniform. One by one, the boy searched the corpse's trouser pockets and found the wallet. He stood up. Two dark green banknotes. He shoved them into his pocket and was folding the wallet when the man's eyes fell on a colour photo. "Give it to me," he said. And he stretched out his hand.

"There is nothing inside," said the boy.

He smiled mockingly and gave it to the man. The man opened the wallet and stared at the picture. There were two children with colourful and cheerful clothes. One had naughty eyes, and the other one a shy smile. The photo had been cut at the edges to fit the wallet size. The man pulled the photo out and wanted to put it in his pocket when he noticed the writing on the back. He swallowed his saliva and turned the photo over.

On it was written: هذه الوردتين ¹

1 This Arabic phrase means 'these two roses'

Haircut

It is my sister's wedding night.

We leave the front before noon to be home by the evening. Mehran, Majid, and me. We have two days leave: half a day for the trip home, half for the return trip, and one evening for the wedding.

When we arrive in Ahvaz, it is already noon, sultry and hot. The hood of Mehran's uncle's green car is shining in the midday sun. I tell Majid: "Give me my bag, I'll carry it myself."

Mehran's uncle is pouring water into the radiator when he raises his head and sees us, as if someone suddenly told him that we were heading towards him from the other side of the road. Mehran starts walking faster. His uncle puts the water can down and opens his arms and both burst out crying. Uncle pats Mehran on the back and says: "What a tragedy, what a tragedy."

I take a step back. Majid puts my bag down and places his thumb and index finger at the corner of his eyes and weeps silently. I step back and tears well up in my eyes.

The car moves off. Mehran sits on the front seat. Majid and I sit in the back, each clinging to the window on his side. I have travelled this road many times. Since the war began, many had moved to cities farther away from the front. I take off my boots and lean my head back against the headrest. I tell Majid, "I'm taking a nap."

I am so embarrassed I can hardly utter a word. Although years have passed and I am sure Uncle will not bring it up to my face, he knows everything. He knows that I continue to send letters to my sister, Mitra, and that Sarah, who is Mitra's best friend goes to our house and reads the letters.

That particular day, Mehran's uncle had put his hand on our bell and had not let go. He had found my letter inside Sarah's chemistry textbook and had rushed to our house at noon sharp. As I opened the door, he removed his hand from the bell and firmly slapped my ear, knocking me to the ground. He had sat on my chest punching me hard in the face. Now he had every right not to hug me.

There are salt fields on both sides of the road as far as the eye could see. Wasteland. The metal electricity pylons are passing fast. One is tall with wide shoulders: the groom. The next one is shorter with a metal skirt: the bride. Groom, bride, groom, bride, groom.

It is my sister's wedding night.

After hugging and kissing my parents, I go to my room and close the door. From my bookshelf, I pick up the third book from the left. I find her letter in the book, as agreed. I read hastily. My mother knocks on the door. "Hurry up. Did you see your suit?" I put the letter back in place and put the book back on the shelf. "I saw it, mum," I say. "I'm coming". Then, I open the closet door and see the white suit. It shines with newness and cleanliness. I take my towel and underwear and go to the bathroom.

I take off these heavy and rough clothes and throw them in the red laundry tub in the right corner of the bathroom. I turn the shower on. She had written that nothing can separate us. She had written: I want you, I want you, I want you. I tell Dad to talk to Majid's uncle tonight at the party. It's only two months to the end of my military service. It will be over in the blink of an eye. I rub the soap on my body. The scent of soap fills my nose. She had written: kiss you, kiss you, kiss you.

We kissed once. In the yard of our house. I opened the gate and she asked, "Excuse me, is Mitra home?" and came in. When I closed the door, we stood there, watching each other. I held out my hand and she put her hand in mine. My heart was pounding. She glanced at the closed door of the entrance hall, leaned forward and stood on her toes, brushing her lips against mine. And I was amazed at her boldness, and at the pleasure of her kiss, and at the way she moved her lips away that I hadn't noticed. She had then rushed into the house.

I turn off the tap. I stand in front of the steamed mirror and apply shaving cream to my face. Someone knocks on the door. I should hurry. Sarah has been here all day before we arrived and has helped mum set the wedding table. We need to take a moment to exchange a glance beyond a blink of an eye. The steam gradually leaves the mirror surface. I have become an old man in the mirror. White-bearded. Like Grandpa. I slide the razor and the skin appears from under the layers of foam.

She has written that she would go to the hairdresser's with Mitra. She has written what a happy day will be the day when you and I put honey in each other's mouths.

Another knock at the door.

I turn the shower on again. My father's voice comes from behind the door. "Hurry up, Son. The bride arrives in a moment and you are still..."

Immersed in a tulle bridal gown, the bride will arrive with her husband who, in his black suit, will be more handsome than ever.

Women will cheer. Sarah will get out of the rear door of the bride's car, and our eyes will meet under the rain of sweets and confetti. I dry my body quickly, put on my towel robe and come out. My mother has put her hair up into a fancy bun. She places her hand atop her mouth, closes her eyes and lets out a loud zaghrouta. She has applied eye shadow. Half green, half blue.

I feel shy and go back into my room to get ready. I pick up the comb and stand in front of the mirror. When she gets out of the bride's car, I will tell her with my eyes: kiss you, kiss you, kiss you.

I comb my hair backward.

Yesterday, Saleh cut my hair. He used to help his father in his barbershop, since he was a teenager. Now, with a small number of tools, Saleh is the battalion's hairdresser. I took off my undershirt and sat on the green ammunition box. Next to the water tanker.

Mehran knelt down in front of us, on the ground, and said, "Hopefully we will celebrate your wedding soon!" and winked. The world knows about our story, not to mention her cousin Mehran! Saleh took the scissors and the comb out of the small, clean bag that he guarded like his life. Mehran said, "Hey, you care too much for him! You cut my hair with clippers."

Saleh replied: "Did it do you any harm? You got engaged immediately after that haircut!" When Mehran went on leave last month, he got engaged. Saleh took the small rectangular mirror out of the bag. He breathed onto it and cleaned it with the edge of his undershirt and gave it to me.

He continued, "For your wedding, I will *inshallah* give you a very nice cut…" He then gently pulled the edge of the scissors over his own neck "…from the base!". He started cutting my hair. The boys gathered around us little by little. The night was calm, and we were far enough away from the danger zone. Majid brought the water canister from the latrine and started to play it like a drum, singing my favourite wedding song. Boys clapped and rejoiced. Muhammad stood up and shook his upper body. Majid was beating on the canister and singing. Muhammad kept jumping up and down; clapping his hands together and repeating the refrain.

At noon, Mehran and I had gone to the city. We made a phone call to inform my mother that I would be home the next evening before the ceremony began. "You called just in time," she said as soon as she picked up the phone, "Come tell your sister, who wears black on her rehearsal dinner? What's wrong with a green dress?"

Mitra's voice could be heard, saying "Mom! Don't be so upset." Mum said: "My God, have you ever seen anyone wearing black in their rehearsal dinner? She asks me not to be upset. But she is the one who makes me upset."

I heard the sound of mwah and mum had said, "May I die for you darling. It's for your own sake. You'll be looking at your photos in a couple of years' time and will regret it," Then she said in the mouthpiece: "See? She fooled me with a kiss." And I had asked laughingly, "Why black?" Mum had said, "Tell me about it! She thinks it's chic. She wants to be different from everyone."

While Saleh cut my hair, Muhammad stood in front of me, his chest trembling. He clasped his wrists together and sang the refrain with pouty lips.

Uncle taps on the steering wheel and sighs loudly. Majid is awake. He leans his head against the window. I softly call his name: "Majid"

He doesn't look back.

"What time is it, Majid?"

"We'll be there in two hours," Mehran says.

Uncle is holding the steering wheel with one hand, tapping on his thigh with the other. "Alas!" Silence falls. "May I die before I get there. How am I going to face them?" And then he begins to sing:

"You were so young for death, O boy, O boy, O boy

The shroud became your wedding suit, O boy, O boy, O boy"

Majid bursts into tears. He covers his face with a handkerchief and cries loudly. Uncle is sobbing.

"Didn't you think your mum is waiting, O boy, O boy, O boy

Didn't you think the bride is yearning, O boy, O boy, O boy

I didn't know you won't be coming back,

You don't know what you did to my soul"

I shrink into myself. Tears run down my face involuntarily. I touch my hair.

Saleh put a new blade in the razor and trimmed my sideburns and around my neck. The sun had set. The boys had dispersed, tired of dancing and drumming. Saleh was patiently tidying up his haircut set in the small bag.

"Pour water on your body", Mehran said. The dream of tomorrow's long shower with fragrant soap and warm water came to my mind.

Saleh's mood was no different from his other days. He was neither happier nor sadder. He had neither felt anything might happen nor had his face lit up.

Mehran got up and said, "My uncle will pick us up from Ahvaz tomorrow." My heart trembled. I said, "your uncle?" He tapped my bare arm and said, "Uncle is not scary. Is he?" Muhammad came out of the makeshift toilet and said, "I left the water" And bent down to pick up the canister. Saleh picked up his bag and said, "Lucky you! Your future father-in-law is picking you up. If you are still unhappy, go throw yourself into the…".

He hadn't finished his sentence when the whistling sound of mortar filled the air. We hit the ground. The sound became deafening. The mortar hit somewhere. The dust rose.

I opened my right eye. I slowly opened my fist. I had dipped my nails in my flesh and had four crescents in my palm. A warm liquid penetrated the thick fabric of my combat pants and its moisture reached the skin. I thought it might be blood. I could hear the boys running towards me. I was alive. I turned my eyes to the side. The water tanker was riddled with shrapnel, and water was flowing from its holes. Majid shook Saleh, who had fallen to the ground, face down. He grabbed his shoulder and arm and rolled him over. His eyes were half open and blood was still spurting from somewhere above his ear. It slid down his neck and into his blue undershirt, which was soaked with sweat.

I shook my foot. It moved. My left hand. Good. My right hand. All unhurt. I sat up.

Muhammad was crumpled on the canister and blood was spilling out of his back. Mehran fell to his knees and shouted, "Oh God."

I got up. My legs were weak. It was a very close call. I walked a few steps away from the boys. Medics ran towards the perforated tanker. I was petrified. I tried to step faster and walked away. I was scared to death. The sound of sobs came from afar.

Uncle says: "We decorated the entire house of Mr. Amini with lighting yarn last night."

I whisper: "Thank you." I want to add: "I hope I can make it up to you" but I realise it is nonsensical to say this to a man who had caught his daughter with me. He sighs. The palm groves pass us quickly right and left. Uncle speeds up. Majid opens his eyes and asks: "Did we pass Borazjan?"

I say, "Sleep tight!", but I regret saying it. Majid is deep in thought. He has lost his best friend, Muhammad.

Uncle says: "Yes, we did."

Mehran says: "Drive more slowly Uncle. What's the point of arriving early?"

I am impatient to arrive. I tie my boot laces tight. Majid puts on his boots and ties the laces loose. Uncle turns left in the first square. People are walking in the streets, shops open: Grocery shops, drug stores, fabric stores, fishmongers, hairdressers. None of them know that Saleh is dead, that Muhammad is dead.

We make another turn. Left, first street, the first house on the right. We stop at Uncle's house. "Would you like to come to our house, or shall we go direct to Mr. Amini's?"

Mehran says: "Let's go". Majid says: "Let's go".

I open the door and say: "Thank you". Our house is seven doors away. I can see the light decorations from here. The gate is open. I say: "You could have rested a little bit, it's too early..." and eat the rest of my words. Your friends have come to your sister's wedding, you fool! And you tell them to stay at their home and rest?

I take long quick steps, but it is rude if I walk ahead of them. We arrive at the gate. My dad is greeting my uncle. He hasn't seen me yet. Mehran's uncle moves one step forward. Dad says "Welcome, where is my son?" I take a step forward, but Uncle stands between me and Dad. Mehran's tears flow on his cheeks and through his thin beard. My mum who was hugging my aunt sees us. I want to go towards her, but Mehran moves one step to the left and blocks my way. Uncle hugs my dad and says: "I am sorry, Mr Amini, I'm sorry."

Mum screams and hits herself in the face. Guests rush out of the house. My uncle holds my dad who nearly collapses into his arms. Dad wants to say something. His mouth is half-open, but no sound comes out of his throat. Whatever direction I aim to go; someone is blocking me. In the middle of a chic and well-scented crowd, with shiny dresses, expensive suits, red ties, jet black shoes and high heels, my mum is screaming: "They killed my son, they killed my son…"

I turn back toward the street. The bride's car decorated with yellow and pink ribbons enters the street, flashing and honking. Mitra steps out of the car, covered in lace and glitter. Her husband is more handsome than ever in a black suit. Sarah opens the back door and gets out. I want our eyes to meet. Even for one moment, but they have killed me. Yesterday, after the haircut.

Divine Signs: Profane Bodies

As soon as I sat down in the bus, I had second thoughts about going. I speculated that he might be a fortune-teller, exorcist or the like. Someone who claimed that he had powers over the motion of divine signs or, who knows, could meld them together. The bus stopped. The station bench was flashing in the scorching sun. Any desire I had to get off evaporated. He couldn't be planning on scamming me. My appearance indicated that I was penniless, war-stricken. Our mutual friend had told him: "He is a writer".

What nonsense!

A bony dark-skinned waiter placed two cups of tea on the table. A long column of ash dangled from his cigarette. His lips still holding the cigarette, he said: "Here you are". The ash fell on to the table next to the Turkish glass cup.

He said: "I'll fix it right away".

The man asked: "Are you really a writer or just dreaming of becoming one?"

The waiter used the napkin he carried on his shoulder to wipe the table. Flies flew away. He spread the ash all over the table. The flies came back and fearlessly sat there again.

I said: "Currently, my situation is... but one day I will write about the time that we had a shop that sold sugar, cubed sugar and tea. I used to sit among the green and red tins of aromatic Indian tea and read books."

For a moment, I thought he was sneering at me. I looked at him. The traces could still be seen on his lips. I didn't continue. He took a drag on his cigarette. All of a sudden, I was dripping with sweat. He looked at me in a questioning manner, prompting me to resume.

I said, "Currently, nothing. I am unemployed".

He said quietly: "Currently, everyone is either fighting or is displaced by the war. But if you have the guts, I may have a job for you".

I said: "It depends on what type of job it is".

The ceiling fan was wobbling. It made a rattling sound every time it rotated and reached a certain point. Inadvertently, I said, "Our fans were British made. They turned as smoothly as a pinwheel the whole summer. When our shop was hit by a mortar, the fan was stuck under the rubble. One blade was left protruding like a hand calling for help. The ants swarmed on the sugar and sugar cubes. They collected enough food for the next hundred years."

"It's one of the blessings of war", he said.

I pretended I hadn't heard him. He bent his head. His beard touched his chest.

He said, "Not bad, but if you want to write, write something extraordinary."

The word extraordinary astonished me. He took a sugar cube from the steel sugar bowl, held it in front of my eyes and said, "There you are, sugar!"

He dropped the sugar into his cup. A few bubbles rose to the surface and burst. He added: "The war will end. Shiploads of sugar and tea will arrive. Write about something that we've lost. Something which will never return". He then stirred his tea with the small dirty tarnished spoon which might have been golden when new. His words shook me, but I felt uneasy that he was able to see things more deeply than me. I contemplated that I would surely reach those deeper layers as I started to write. I felt the urge to say I know what to write and that my friend should not have told you that I write and stuff. But I was unable to utter a word. Only my lips parted a little. He drank his tea and left some change on the table. We rose and walked to the door. I stood by the Coleman water cooler. I heard my mum warning us not to drink water after tea or our teeth would crack. I wanted to pray for her soul, but changed my mind. I remembered that we had a Coleman with large green flower patterns on it at home. What kind of flower is green? I have no idea! There was always a shiny steel glass next to it. We used to cycle to the ice factory every day to buy ice. We wrapped the ice block in gunny bags and secured it to the rear rack with straps. The burning sun would melt half of the block away before we got home. The cold water slipped off my teeth and went down my throat.

"Water has no taste in these plastic cups". I said.

I looked back. He was stealthily weighing me up. I splashed the last drops of water at the dirty wall tiles.

"Instead, the water is sweet here' he said.

"Instead of what? Us being war-stricken?" I said.

It seemed my words did the trick. He sulked. I dropped the cup. It fell and remained suspended above the floor, held there by a dirty string attached to its handle. I felt angry at myself. The glass was wobbling. Why should I remain imprisoned by these memories for so long? Don't I have anything of substance to tell this stranger? We headed out. As I opened my mouth to say goodbye he asked: "How is it that no one was martyred in your family?"

"I'm afraid! It just didn't happen", I said.

He made me feel as if I owed something.

"You are not afraid of the dead, are you?" he asked.

"Afraid? I dragged a hundred people out of the rubble during bombardments", I said.

What nonsense!

He said he had to go and wrote his address on a piece of paper with a red pen.

The bus driver shouted, "All change". I pulled out the piece of paper from my pocket. Crumpled and sweaty. I asked the driver for directions and walked. It was a big place. I walked past white rusty fences until I arrived at the gate. It occurred to me that it might be a hospital. The guard gestured me to stop. He glared at me and leaped out of his sentry box.

– Stay where you are. Who do you want to see?

– Mr. Rasouli

– Who gave you the address?

Gradually, his tone became more aggressive.

– He did.

– Why do you want to see him? Don't move, stay there!

A refrigerated truck arrived. The guard spoke on the radio and opened the gate. The truck drove in. It turned round the building and was hidden from sight. The building was a large concrete structure. The guard spoke on his radio again and signalled to me to come closer. The building had had a large sign which had been removed. The buckled fluorescent units behind the signboard had been left above the entrance. A sergeant and a soldier emerged from a smaller building which was nearer, to the left of the big building, and approached me.

The sergeant ordered: "Turn around, face the wall".

The soldier searched me. I tried to explain that an acquaintance had given me the damned address and that I might have come to the wrong address.

– If you have come to the wrong address, how come you know the name Rasouli?

They handcuffed me and indicated that I move ahead. We walked to the smaller building which looked like an office building with its long corridor full of metal filing cabinets. The soldier opened the door to the first room. I was completely baffled.

– Remove his handcuffs!

They pushed me inside and locked the door behind me. I sat on the grey carpet and took my shoes off, without feeling embarrassed about the big hole in my sock. The odour from my feet was overwhelming. I looked round the empty room. It was cool and quiet and had a small window, the panes of which were painted brown. I reflected that I had wasted so many years that a few more hours wouldn't do any harm. No sound could be heard from outside. Suddenly I trembled at the thought that I might have to spend a few years in this room. I consoled myself with the hope that it was impossible. I lay on my side, supported my head with one hand and closed my eyes. A voice inside my head said: It is possible! I opened my eyes. Ants were struggling to move through the carpet pile. When they encountered one another, it looked as if they were exchanging very serious words and went on their way. They were carrying parts of an insect limb towards a hole in the wall. I realised that this is not a lawless state. They will ask me a couple of questions and let me go. The voice in my head said, "It is not a lawless state!" I followed the ant trail and arrived at the dried body of an insect. It wasn't clear what type of insect it had been. I cursed my friend who had introduced me to this fellow. Son of a bitch. If he knew of any job, he would have recommended his own family and relatives. It was written on the door of his father's butchery: "And That Man Shall Have Nothing But What He Strives For". Yet, the only thing he did was to collect the cash from the takings every evening. Bastard. Worker ants persistently cut parts of the insect body and carried it away. I wondered if worker ants knew they were workers.

I heard the key turning in the lock. I jumped up. I saw my acquaintance shaking hands with the sergeant. I breathed a sigh of relief. I bent down and tied my shoelaces. My contact patted me on the shoulder. I stood upright. The sergeant had gone.

"It's a bit complicated here", he said.

I acted as if nothing had happened. He patted me on the shoulder again to urge me to move. An unpleasant smell emanated from his body or may be from his clothes. We stopped between two buildings. He lit a cigarette and handed it to me. He lit another one for himself.

"You did well to come here", he said.

I looked around. The asphalt was shining under the sun. I pledged myself not to say anything unless absolutely necessary.

He looked older than the day I met him for the first time. Having smoked half the cigarette, he threw it down and slowly crushed it under his feet. I took the last drag and threw down mine. With the tip of his shoe, he pressed one of the cigarette butts against the wall. I thought its guts would have spilled out if it were an insect.

We climbed ten to twelve stairs and entered the bigger

building. A diagonal column of dim light poured through the round air vent. Dust particles were dancing slowly inside the light column. We were in a hall with doors on either side. There was a third large door facing us. Voices could be heard on radios. Someone came and whispered something in my acquaintance's ear. He placed his hand on the back of my shoulder, prompting me to move. He opened the big door. A rather stout man in green military uniform stared at my acquaintance with his tiny green discontented eyes. My associate moved away and took the man to one side. I could see his profile; his big hook nose and his massive beard.

He said: "No, it's wrong". And moved a bead along his rosary.

My acquaintance stated that he needed more staff and that he fully trusted me. I surmised it was probably an ammunition storage or weapon repair facility. The man kept murmuring something and moving his rosary beads. My acquaintance mentioned that I had come from the war zone and had lost everything. There was a huge fridge door in front of me. I thought this might be a cold storage facility for meat and fruit and felt hungry. My acquaintance was gradually raising his voice. The bearded man stressed that he wouldn't permit it. Suddenly, the acquaintance shouted, "You have never dared to step inside. You can't tell me what to do or what not to do". He then turned his back on him and angrily signalled for me to follow.

I tried not to look at the bearded man who was standing there motionless. It occurred to me that finding a job was not worth this much trouble. He pressed the large metal handle. I felt the gentle touch of a cold breeze on my face. There were large boxes carelessly covered with canvas on both sides. The thought came to me that now that I am in an ammunition storage unit, I could take some bullet casings or other useless items for my sister's children to play with. They had abandoned their toys at home if there was any home left by now. For a moment, I saw the world crumbling on my head. He was right to say that we had lost everything. There was another large steel door in front of us. My acquaintance entered a code into the keypad. Half of his body was reflected on the polished door. Someone opened the door. An unexpectedly cold, foul smell numbed my whole body. It felt as if I had turned on the living room air conditioner at noon and smelled the lizard that had died between the blades. We stepped inside. The heat followed us in and a thin fog emerged. The man who had opened the door fastened it securely behind me. The room was cavernous. Everything was dark and grey.

– Come forward, don't be afraid.

There were no weapons. I could see a pile of unrecognisable objects a few meters away. Old clothes were heaped up on another side. Men were moving in different directions. It was not clear what they were doing. The light from the fluorescent tubes was not bright enough for such a massive place. My foot hit a heavy box. It was big – as long as a human. It didn't look empty. A person was lying in the box, a real person covered in blood. I pressed my eyelids together and opened them again. It was just the head and torso. Half a man covered in blood. A young voice said, "Haven't you found a leg for this one?"

I was paralysed. The voice said, "Put it in and close the lid". I slowly lifted my head up. The heap of objects gradually took shape before my eyes. The fog was gone. I gathered all my strength and moved one step closer. A heap of human body, a mountain of men.

Naked. Blended. Intertwined. Deformed. With twisted bones. Hand, leg, head, with frozen streams of blood. A complete body, intact, clean, with skin the colour of moonlight but no head. A trunk turned blue, bruised, its head under another torso. A hip that led to no leg. Torn apart and scabbed. Severed limbs, without a torso, without a body. Hand, leg, foot, arm, wrist, a faceless head.

"What is this place?" I screamed but my voice choked in my throat and clawed at my larynx like a faceless hand. All of a sudden, all the lifeless limbs started to move. Fear penetrated deep into my flesh like a sharp cleaver. Someone climbed on to the heap, threw down a hand and commanded his fellow worker: "Throw the arms here".

"What is this place?" I screamed, and my voice spun round in my head, around the cold storage and in my mind ten times. I felt a warmth behind me. I turned round. My acquaintance hugged me. I burst into tears. I was unable to stand and kept slipping out of his arms. He held me firm and whispered in my ear, "This place is where we meld divine signs together. Say you can't work here. Go out and never look back. Don't tell anybody about it. When the dust has settled in a few years' time, write this. I won't be alive by then, but I want you to write it."